The Recession Won't Last But Salvation Will

Published by Six Hearts Publishing

Six Hearts
publishing

First USA Edition – 2011
The Recession Won't Last But Salvation Will

SUMMARY
The Recession Won't Last But Salvation Will

If you are like most people, you've either been impacted by the recession or you know someone who has been. Millions have lost their jobs, homes and relationships while healthy individuals have become ill, due to stress, fear and anxiety. The suicide rate is on the rise. As long as we are in this world we will be surrounded by negativity, but what matters most is our game plan to stay ahead and maintain a positive outlook on life, despite the damaging effects of the economic turmoil.

The word of God is the only truth and this book contains promises of God's Protection, Provision and Deliverance as recorded in Jeremiah 29:11: *"For I know the plans I have for you," declares the Lord, "plans to prosper you and not to harm you, plans to give you hope and a future."* This is just one of many of His promises, but most believers struggle with unbelief. This brief documentation will give you courage and strength to withstand whatever challenges you might be faced with and give you the tools to fight off the crippling fear that plagues us daily.

Read about the hero in the story, Ray Gordon, Vice President of IT Enterprises, forced to layoff 145 employees and in that same day was brought to shame and humiliation and learned later that job security is a thing of the past. The author agrees that Network Marketing and home-based businesses are the way of the future. "Let us embrace our God given talent, fight off the recession with a vengeance and take back what is rightfully ours.

Published in the United States of America.
No part of this book may be used or reproduced in any manner
without the written permission of the publisher

Cover and Text pages designed by: Huntley Burgher
Photography: Don Parchment
Written by: Nina Hart
Edited by: Dr. Garth Rose
Inspired by: Dr. Jason Campbell

Published by: Six Hearts Publishing
10741 Pine Lodge Trail, Davie, Florida 33328
www.sixheartspublishing.com
February 2011

ISBN 978-0-9845767-2-2

Library of Congress Cataloging-in-Publication Data

All scripture quotations are taken from the King James version
of the Holy Bible.

Printed in the United States of America

DEDICATION
The Recession Won't Last But Salvation Will

This book is dedicated to every person who is willing to share God's promises or give a helping hand, to encourage those who have lost jobs, homes and relationships during this recession.

ACKNOWLEDGEMENTS

It was a beautiful September evening when I received a call from my eldest son, Dr Jason Campbell, "Mom I've been thinking about this over the past couple of days and I believe you should write a book about the recession. Here are my thoughts, lately you've been travelling quite a bit, so just write a couple chapters while you're flying and before you know it, you would have written your next book."

My response was, "J, I never really thought about that, but I've got to focus on marketing the books I have in print right now. Maybe down the road, but you know I have to feel it before I can write about it, so we'll see, but not now.

I flew to New York in October and about half way on the journey, I heard my son's voice echoing in my head, "Write a couple chapters while you're flying." I tried hard to shut it out, but I couldn't. I prayed and asked the Lord to occupy my thoughts and it was a while before it started to come together. Well by the time I returned home, I'd written two chapters.

I flew to Jamaica in November as I had two speaking engagements, first time in 32 years away from my children for Thanksgiving. Wow! My youngest daughter Trish-Ann, who's in the US Navy, was not home either, so it made it a little easier for me to handle. I stayed with my sister, Julin and her husband, Desbert James; they're on fire for the Lord, so I shared the idea about my new book, *The Recession Won't Last But Salvation Will.* To this day, I'm not sure what they did, but all I know I was glued to the room for about five days until I completed the book.

I knew for sure that the Lord was with me through the entire process. Sometimes I would read to my sister in the night and I didn't remember writing some of what I read. The saying, 'Let go and let God, is what transpired with this little book!

Special Thanks to Jason, who planted the seed, that God gave life. To Trish, who the Lord had call me in Jamaica and gave me the title for the sermon, Fire- Proof vs Recession- Proof, and also the scripture. To my other four supporters for life; Leighton, Leneen, David and Paul. To all my brothers and sisters who have lent their support in one way or another. Much love and gratitude to my sister Julin, who has been my greatest encourager and who would not sleep without hearing the story read each night. To my brother in law, Desbert James who was instrumental in arranging the 400+ home based businesses at the back of the book. To my friend Joe Reid, one of my mentors, who has succeeded in Network Marketing, (try to find Joe in the story). Jim Fobair, your success is largely based on your commitment to serve the Lord.

Dr. Garth Rose, I can always rely on your support, thank you! Huntley Burgher, thank you for being committed to the industry. To my family and friends who came forward to help make this publication possible; Edward Harmon, Jolie Abru, Irene Korge, Norma Jean Abraham, Dr. Rudy Moise, Joe Reid, Noel Crooks, Desiree Mufson, Dr. Nsombi Jaja, June Johnson, Sandra & Mark Davis, Marcia McPherson, Dacia Riley, Lloyd & Mauva Smith, Marjorie Kellier, Audrey Watkis, Carmel Moise. If there is anyone who has helped with this publication that I have not mentioned, please know that my sincere appreciation goes to all.

Chapter 1

"Excuse me Ms. Rigg, did you get the communication out to our entire staff? "

"Yes Mr. Gordon, I did."

As I drove home that evening I dreaded facing the mandatory meeting scheduled to address the massive layoff the following morning at 9:00 AM. This company has a total of 375 employees, but based on the economic downturn the decision was made, and being the Vice President of the company, I was responsible to layoff 145 mid and lower grade employees. The CEO, Mr. Owen Sinclair, would layoff the five high level grade employees. What a condition? I knew when I was promoted eight years ago to VP, that I would be literally responsible for running the company, so why was I so surprised? Mr. Sinclair calls me his right hand man, as no decisions are made without him first consulting with me. If I can be honest, Mr. Sinclair wears the title but I do the majority of the work. However, I don't complain because they pay me well.

It might sound crazy but I really love my job, demanding as it is; I love it, as stressful as it is I love it. I even love the confrontations with my boss, as I learn how to be bold and to speak up respectfully.

After graduating from the University of Miami twenty five years ago, this was my first job interview and I nailed it. I majored in Computer Science as I was always intrigued by computers, and knew that one day it would be the primary source of communication in the world. My goal was to work for a company that built computers and supplied all the accessories, so when I landed the job with IT Enterprises, a Japanese based company, I counted my blessings.

Over twenty five years, I have watched the company grow from generating sales of $565,000 per year to $1.5 billion. When I got on board, there were 15 employees and now we have 375. I have had 3 CEO's but Mr. Sinclair has lasted the longest. I have absolutely no complains about the company, they have been good to me as I have been good to them. Being in management makes me exempt, so I work anywhere from 60-70 hours per week. I get my work ethics from my mother; having lost my father to cancer when I was only 10 years old my mother did an amazing job raising me. She emphasized the importance of a good education. College was not an option and even though I did not pursue medicine like she wanted me to, she told me that as long as I graduated and got a good job I could count on her support. As for her, she was a book-keeper when my father passed, and she worked with the company while they funded her accounting degree. Today she's with the same company and is one of their leading CPA's and at 56 she's working on her doctorate in accounting. So based on how I was raised, I don't move from job to job. I will stay with the same company until I retire; by that time, the benefits will be stacked high. By then, the 401K can pay off the balance of my mortgage and I will be able to maintain my life-style on my pension alone.

Back in 1985 my annual starting salary was $45,000, since then I have averaged approximately 10-15 percent annual increase, except for the past two years, making my salary a little over $200,000 annually. I have so much to be thankful for. Often times when I drive home from work I would pray and thank God for his blessings and this evening was no different.

"Lord I just want to lift you up and thank you for the many blessings. Despite the tension and the gloom over tomorrow's meeting, I pray for wisdom and understanding to do the right thing. Lord especially being raised by a single mother, my heart is so full and I'm so concerned about how the heads of the single parent households will manage when they lose their only source of income."

As the tears welded in my eyes, a still small voice whispered in my ear,

Philippians 4:19
"But my God shall supply all your need according to his riches in glory by Christ Jesus."

Then suddenly calm came over me and I continued to pray;

"Lord help me to trust you more, love you more

and serve you more. Thank you for my beautiful family; my precious wife Virginia and our two wonderful children Ryan and Rebecca. Please watch over them and cover them with your blood, keep them safe from all harm and danger. Thank you for providing a gorgeous home, food to eat and clothes to wear. Thank you that we're able to give back to your work, Lord I thank you for mine and Virginia's jobs. In a time when people are losing jobs, homes and relationships you've protected and prospered us, and for that we thank you. "

Right as I concluded the prayer I drove through the entrance to my neighborhood, I cruised along as I admired the homes on both sides, "Wow, I should have bought pre-construction when these homes were selling for $650,000!" But sometimes when you wait around to make decisions, it usually cost you. When we bought our home 4 years ago we paid $2 million, but at the time they were being sold for $2.5 million so we had instant equity before the ink even dried on the closing documents. Two years later we're totally upside down, and even worse than that, we couldn't even sell if we wanted to. One of the things that caused me great concern was that 'Negative Arm' mortgage that the banker suggested, only a pity we didn't look more into it. That's what happens sometimes when you trust someone. If I were to do it over again, I'd be doing my own research and make a timely decision instead of following the advice of the 'experts'. Because of that advice, for three years we were paying $4,600 per month and now the payment has almost doubled to $7,200.00, because of that negative arm that many folks got stuck with. Such a pity this was not fully explained, but we're fortunate that we can afford that type of payment. There are many who had to succumb to foreclosure, based on these sub-prime mortgages. But I really did not expect the market to crash so quickly, now that the real estate bubble has burst, our $2 million dollar property is now valued at $950,000, and we're still paying taxes on the original sales price. That's something I'm going to have to contest as the taxes should be based on appraised value. However the good news is; we can manage as Virginia and I both have good paying jobs, but these properties might never go back to the inflated value, which is not good for us and most people, but it's a global melt down and millions are being impacted.

Subprime mortgages were a total disaster. Lenders were approving people who didn't even have jobs, so it was only a matter of time for things to come tumbling down, and the sad part is everyone pays, both the good and the bad!

It's funny how the experts have motivated us over the years to invest in Real Estate as it's a sound investment, but it doesn't seem that sound anymore. God help us if Virginia or I should ever lose our jobs!

Our lot was sitting on an acre in a cul-de-sac, which made it safe for the kids to play out front under the supervision of Ena, their live-in nanny. She did not let them out of her sight. Ryan was seven and Rebecca five. They were both loving and kind children, and sharp as a tack! As I unlocked the side door to the garage Rebecca ran towards me to get her teddy bear hug while Ryan ran up to give me a high-five. The kids did not sense that I was not goofing around as I used to, they ran back to the family room to watch Peacebe and the Heartwatch, their favorite cartoon that teaches family values from a tender age.

When I greeted Virginia, she sensed the tension and knew immediately that something was wrong, and with a concerned look she asked.

"Honey, what's going on at the office?"

"You don't want to know, tomorrow is the big day

and as it stands the layoff is estimated at about 150 employees, of which I have to personally layoff 145 of them."

"Wow, that would make me real nervous, and what's up with the other five, who are those?"

" Do you think for a minute that I'm not nervous? The other five are the high level grade employees that Mr. Sinclair himself will terminate. If I didn't have 25 years invested in this company and didn't have such great responsibilities I would be pacing the floor right now. But God is gracious and is not slack concerning his promise, so I don't think I personally have anything to worry about. I literally run this company Virginia, believe it or not, I am the man!"

Shaking her head she questions; "Ray, aren't you the VP of the company, which means you're high, high level, right next to the CEO? I believe the earning of the 145 that you'll be laying off might not even add up to the salaries of the 5 top earners. I would be very concerned right about now if I were you. Yeah! I would be sending up some serious prayer requests to God. However, I know that God can do anything, but to tell you the truth, I'm not feeling too good about it."

"Virginia, the truth is I'm more concerned for some of these single parent households, how will they manage especially seeing that jobs are so hard to find? How will they provide for their children?"

Virginia replied, "Honey, this recession is truly a test of our faith, we need to stop putting our trust in these jobs, and all this material stuff, and put out trust completely in the Lord. Ray, I can't express what I'm feeling right now, but I just have to spend some time in prayer.

Virginia seemed spaced out for a minute and it

seemed as though she was having a conversation in the spirit. Then I heard her say in a soft tone, "Yes Lord, I know Lord, thank you for the assurance Lord.

John 14:27
"Peace I leave with you, my peace I give to you, not as the world gives. Do not let your hearts be troubled and do not be afraid."

She came over and embraced me, "Honey, don't worry God will see you through, but I do believe that this recession will force us to create our own jobs, so we can stop depending solely on a 9-5 job."

"How is that possible?" I asked.

"Honey it's the information age, it's the age of Network Marketing."

My defenses were up, "I can't even begin to fathom that stuff Virginia, it's definitely not for me. The folks who get into that sort of thing, are kind of like 'Rejects' and cannot find real jobs."

Virginia did not like my response. "What is a real job anyway, are we talking about the real jobs that folks are losing by the millions. Let's keep it real Ray , job security is a thing of the past. "

I found that comment somewhat annoying, and I replied, "I don't agree with you Virginia."

"You might not agree with me Ray, but the facts are the facts; Network Marketing generates billions of dollars and creates jobs for thousands of people every year. People need to get with the program and be more receptive to looking into Network Marketing or some type of home based business. As for me, if I should ever lose my job I'd be calling up my friend in New York who's been trying to get me to look at a 'Weight-Loss Line' for the past six months or so. I have been thinking about it and did some further research and found out that ten of the eleven companies that have earned over a billion dollars are all health and wellness companies. So what does that tell you? This stuff is recession proof. Women are going to find a way to look fine no matter the economic climate and no matter their age."

"OK Virginia, I cannot grasp this Network Marketing/Weight Loss Products concept right now. My entire focus is on tomorrow's meeting, can you please try to understand that?"

"I understand that honey, but I'd encourage you to keep an open mind. Like the saying goes; "The mind is like a parachute, it's only good when it's open.""

"I agree with most of what you've said Virginia, but

when you're as close to this situation as I am, it makes it very difficult."

I didn't sleep well that night and was up at the crack of dawn to have an early devotion. After praying, I showered and got dressed and left for the office around 6:30. I had no appetite for breakfast; I hurriedly left the house and decided to have coffee at the office. You'd think that I owned this company, but I had work to do and was going to pull myself together to get the job done. I walked into the meeting room at 8:30 and found all the chairs were laid out, water to the back of the room and a table stacked high with sealed envelopes next to the podium. Those were; Layoff - Severance Packages. Mr. Sinclair called to apprise me of what was being given in the severance packages - one month salary, plus payments for unused vacation or sick time. Health and life insurance would be terminated that very day.

Employees were informed that by US law, the Consolidated Omnibus Budget Reconciliation Act (COBRA) allowed them to continue their coverage at group rates, plus a 2 percent administration fee. But, they may be able to find a better deal than COBRA, here is the stark reality:

Health Insurance - Coverage may end on the day you're laid off, or shortly thereafter..

Life Insurance - Typically ends on the day you're laid off, and is not covered under COBRA. But, your ex-employer may offer you a continuance option. It usually isn't cheap, and you may be able to find a better deal.

Disability Insurance - The same as life insurance. Alternately, you might be covered by your state unemployment plan for free, but the weekly benefit amount may be less than private plans.

The meeting was called to order by the CEO, Mr. Sinclair. He thanked all the employees for their dedication and assured them that the company would gladly furnish letters of recommendations to anyone who needed them. Lost for words, and not wanting to look awkward, he turned the meeting over to me and immediately left the room.

Chapter 2

I was thrown to the wolves and it was a frightening experience, but I had to embrace it and get the job done. You would believe that we were at a viewing, the place felt morbid. Folks were sobbing and fear was written all over their faces. I noticed that some of the guys had pronounced veins imprinted on their foreheads; it was scary and I raised my hand feeling my forehead to see if I had protruding veins also. The only thing missing from the room was a casket. I realized that before I could say a word I needed to hear from the Lord. Quietly I prayed, "Lord I need you, I need to hear from you right now."

The assurance came from;

2 Timothy 1:7
For God hath not given us the spirit of fear; but of power, and of love, and of a sound mind.

"Thank you Jesus." I cleared my throat and spoke; I was feeling confident and bold enough to carry out the task that I had been assigned to. My address was sincere and from the heart:

"Folks, this is undoubtedly one of the hardest things I have ever been asked to do, I am at a loss for words but the quote that readily comes to mind is; "Where duty calls I must obey." With that said, please know that I empathize with everyone who will be let go today, but I stand here not having answers. But as one of the leaders in this organization, I've been asked to carry out this task. Just last night my wife reminded me that there is no such thing as 'job security' anymore, and this experience is forcing me to agree with her. I wish you all God's blessings!"

One side of me was strong but the compassionate side was ready to break down as I fought to hold back the tears. I needed a handful of tissue to stop the tears from rolling down my cheeks. However, my corporate image surfaced and I pulled on my inner strength.

"The names will be announced in alphabetical order, please come forward when your name is called and receive your severance package, if you have questions regarding this layoff please contact the Human Resource Department."

I commenced the recital of the names........Everyone was angry; One month's salary, with health and life insurance terminating that day. No smiles, the atmosphere was pretty hostile. I was trying hard to get through the names quickly before I was attacked. I was on –R- the next candidate was Jon Reid but affectionately called JR. When the package was handed to him he smiled and said; "Thank you, that means I have three months to triple my income."

Suddenly everyone became quiet and the room that was filled with uproar instantly became still. JR had the floor and he was going to make good use of his one minute of fame.

"Mr. Gordon, it was a pleasure working with you sir, here is my card, you may need it in the future." I quickly took his card and shoved it in my back pocket as JR continued with his speech.

"You might all think I'm crazy, but I've got a bright future ahead, I've been building my Network Marketing business for the past 12 months and a month ago I was able to match my salary. Now that I'll be working it full time, I'll be able to triple my income in a few short months. There's no job security, let's have a committal service for the good ole 9-5..."

At that point two security guards went up and escorted him out of the building. They could not stop the crowd from following him. JR exercised his rights as a law abiding citizen and passed out his information, but more importantly he took the information of approximately 65 individuals who had an interest in hearing more about his business. Of course, some people thought he was crazy but as for me, I found the whole thing very interesting.

Back in the meeting room, I ended the gruesome task of laying off workers and walked swiftly to my office as I tried hard to avoid any discussions with this angry mob. But try as hard as I could, I was unable to dismiss JR from my mind.

With my shoulders drooped and my brain drained, I dialed Ms. Rigg's extension.

"Can you please do me a huge favor and hold all my calls for the next hour unless it's extremely important, I've got some work I have to catch up on and do not wish to be disturbed."

"OK Mr. Gordon, I will hold all your calls, Sir."

I had a chance to cry and de-stress, hoping that there were no hidden cameras in my office. I was all corporate on the outside, but on the inside I was a compassionate, warm, caring type of guy with real emotions. Forty five minutes had quickly flown by when Ms. Rigg buzzed my extension. She was very good at taking orders, so the interruption must be the result of something very important.

"Mr. Gordon, so sorry to interrupt, but I just received a call from Mr. Sinclair requesting a private meeting with you at 3:45 today. He wanted me to call him back to confirm that you will be able to attend the meeting."

"Of course I'll be able to attend the meeting with Mr. Sinclair, I'm sure he wants us to recap today's events, kindly go ahead and confirm."

A light bulb went off in my head and I had a great idea. I was going to surprise Mr. Sinclair and brighten his day. So I spent the rest of the afternoon strategizing and documenting how 225 employees would effectively carry out the responsibilities of the 375 that was once the full staff complement. I knew he was relying on me and despite the downsizing we had to continue with business as usual, everything was going to be mapped out and the implementation was going to be flawless.

A few hours went by and I felt extremely good about the work I did, I couldn't wait to share it with Mr. Sinclair, he was my biggest fan outside of Virginia. Speaking of Virginia, I needed to give her a quick call to let her know that my mission was accomplished. I didn't want to forget, so I immediately called her on her direct line.

"Hi sweetheart, you'd be so proud of me. Just to let you know that the job has been done and I'm getting ready to go into a meeting with my boss." The line went still and I wondered if the call got disconnected.

Then I heard her whisper, "Honey, no matter the outcome, it's important for you to know that I believe in you. I'm always going to be proud of you, no matter what. But right now the Lord wants me to share this verse of scripture with you:

Proverbs 3:6
"In all thy ways acknowledge Him and He will direct your paths."

All the best with your meeting and let's talk at home later, I love you."

I glanced at my watch and gathered all the information regarding the reorganization of IT Enterprises. When Mr. Sinclair and I had meetings in the past, we would always meet at least half an hour early to chit chat about family, politics and sports but this day, I knew we'd only be talking about the massive layoff.

I got all my ammunition together and dashed out of my office, I was standing in front of Mr. Sinclair's door in less than a minute. I knocked on the door and there was no answer, "Hmmm that's strange," I thought. I sat outside his office door going over the work I was about to present to him, I got so caught up with it that I didn't realize when Mr. Sinclair walked up.

It was exactly 3:45. "Strange," I again thought.

Instead of greeting in his usual, casual manner, saying. "Ray what have you got going on today?' He said, "Mr. Gordon, please come with me." That was very strange!

I walked into the office feeling sorry for my boss. For a minute it felt awkward but I was committed to be the one to accentuate the positive and leave the negative behind, so I said; "Sir, I spent the entire afternoon restructuring and organizing a system that will keep us in the game. The cut of 150 employees will not compromise the top performance we've been known for over the past decade, nor will it interfere with our delivery cannel. There will be no room for time wasters, no more goofing off on the job and zero tolerance for errors. My ultimate goal is to create an 'error free' workplace. This plan is designed for the brightest and the best employees, they will be required to double up on their work, with the same amount of pay. At the rate how folks are being laid off, they will be happy to do whatever it takes to secure their jobs. Mr. Sinclair, did you know that sixty-five percent of employees just work so as not to get fired, seventeen percent just work so they can get the job done and believe it or not, only eighteen percent of employees are really passionate about what they do. We want our entire team to be eighteen per-centers!"

When I didn't get a response I thought he was trying to understand the plan, but a quick look in his eyes made it seem as though he was on the verge of a nervous breakdown. So in a concerned tone I asked, "Are you ok, Sir?"

"No, how can I be OK when I'm being forced to layoff my right hand man."

His words went right past me, because even though I always knew that I was his right hand man, I knew he had to be referring to another right hand man, definitely not me.

However, thinking that I understood what he was saying, he continued,

"It took you two hours to layoff one hundred and forty-five people, but it took me all day to layoff just five, you being the last one. You high level grade employees literally run the company."

I was speechless, listless and weak and I instantly had issues with my comprehension skills.

He continued, "I want to thank you for your twenty five years of dedicated service and I know it will be very hard trying to find a replacement for you. Your package includes six months' salary and also full medical benefits for six months. Please call HR if you have any questions regarding the package."

I was outraged. "After twenty five years all I get is six months' salary, I've spent half my life in this God forsaken place and this is my reward! This is unacceptable." The Holy Spirit chimed in;

Ephesians 4:26
"Be angry and sin not."

I remained quiet while Mr. Sinclair got up from his chair and extended his hand.

"Mr. Gordon, you might not believe this, but I did everything to retain you, I had numerous conversations with Mr. Kobayashi, the owner of the company who resides in Japan, but he would not bend. The bottom line is, based on your salary we could outsource your job to twenty workers in India and still be left with a surplus."

I was being compared to blue collar workers who're paid 75 cents an hour. What an insult.

"Be angry and sin not, be angry and sin not, be angry and sin not!"

I knew I had to be obedient to the Holy Spirit, so I tried hard to zip my lips, but I was livid. I could not believe anything I heard and for a moment I thought I was watching a horror movie. I thought about Virginia's spiel on Network Marketing and JR's bold announcement. I felt myself feeling in my back pocket to ensure that I had his card. Then a thought raced through my mind, 'If I had put in 25 years in Network Marketing, I wonder where would I be today?'

I was jolted to my senses by Mr. Sinclair's comment. "Mr. Gordon, have a good day, sir." I looked up and his extended hand was an indication for me to leave. I felt like talking because there was so much I had to say, but his job was done and I needed to go. No celebrations for the eight years when I did the work of the CEO and he received the compensation. No balloons, no cards, no watches, no nothing, but an extended hand waiting for me to leave! I slowly stood up, shook his hand then walked away.

As I walked to my office, a million thoughts were racing through my brain at once and though I felt really terrible about being laid off, that was not my doing, so I know I had to pull myself together and get over myself. But the one thing I really felt bad about was my negative reaction towards Network Marketing. My response to Virginia echoed in my ears, 'Network Marketing is for rejects.'

'Well I must be a reject because Corporate America kicked me to the curb after twenty-five years of dedicated service. What a blow to a man's ego, how on earth do I break this news to my wife?'

A state of depression swept over me and suddenly I felt like a loser. Now that I have lost my job was

I going to lose my family, house and car? I quickly dismissed the negative thoughts and now I needed some reassurance, but one thing I knew for sure my salvation was secure. If I lost everything I worked hard for, I could not lose my salvation because that was one thing that did not cost me anything, it was F-R-E-E! The Holy Spirit reminded me of;

Phil 3:13-14:

Brethren, I count not myself to have apprehended: but this one thing I do, forgetting those things which are behind, and reaching forth unto those things which are before, I press toward the mark for the prize of the high calling of God in Christ Jesus.

As I began to accept the reality that I was no longer the Senior Vice President of IT Enterprises I picked up my name plate and gazed at it for a while, this little piece of wood gave me power and made me feel important, as it made everyone know that I was a man with authority. Today I am stripped of my position and the name plate is meaningless, the authority went through the back door. "Yes Lord, I'm hearing you."

Matthew 6:20
But store up for yourselves treasures in heaven, where moth and rust do not destroy, and where thieves do not break in and steal.

This was highway robbery, but I'm going to trust God that He has a bigger and better plan for my life. As my flesh battled with my spirit I gathered my personal belongings in two boxes that were conveniently placed by my door. I took down my wedding picture and also Ryan and Rebecca's portraits of when they were dedicated and I looked at them long and hard. I spent the last five hours formulating a plan for the continued success of this company, but I did not have a contingency plan to ensure the success of my family. That did not make sense and it definitely was a rude awakening. The Holy Spirit knew my despair and came to my rescue;

Jeremiah 29:11

For I know the plans I have for you," declares the Lord, "plans to prosper you and not to harm you, plans to give you hope and a future.

Yeah, I was going to hold on to this promise, because I know He would not go back on his word and how do I know he would not go back on his word?

Matthew 24:35

Heaven and earth will pass away, but my words will never pass away.

Though I knew that scripture, I needed to hear it now, I finished packing my personal belongings, picked up my shoulders and walked out of the office leaving the hopelessness behind and taking strength and courage with me.

Chapter 3

As I drove home I couldn't stop the tears streaming down my face, the more I wiped them the more they gushed down. In one moment I was strong and in another, I felt weak. I was nervous to face Virginia and have to confess that I was wrong about the security of my job. 'There's no job security, that's a thing of the past,' her words echoed in my ears. A very humbling reminder from the Holy Spirit,

Proverbs 16:18
Pride goeth before destruction, and an haughty spirit before a fall.

Wow! Such a sobering lesson in humility.

"Where did strength and courage go, did they decide to leave? Lord maybe I'm really worried about maintaining our lifestyle that we've comfortably managed for years and suddenly the rug is pulled from under my feet. Maybe I'll have to downsize our lifestyle and move out of the neighborhood to a low income area. What a transformation Lord, it's so much to deal with right now, but I'm ready to do what you want me to do." Then another reminder from the Holy Spirit,

Psalm 23:6
Surely, goodness and mercy shall follow me all the days of my life: and I will dwell in the house of the Lord forever.

So despite what I'm going through, 'Goodness and Mercy' will follow me, God's word says it and I believe it! This was going to help me fight off the spirit of worry. Suddenly my heart was filled with a song my mother would sing when she was facing difficulties and it would just bless her heart. 'Why worry when you can pray? Ttrust Jesus and He will lead the way, don't be like doubtful Thomas, but rest upon His promise, why worry, worry, worry when you can pray.'

I sang and prayed, sang and prayed until my faithless worries were gone. As I pulled up in the garage, with my car packed to capacity with things from my office, Virginia came out and before I even had a chance to turn off the ignition, she leaned over and kissed me on the cheek. "Honey, the Holy Spirit showed me everything, and I don't want you to worry about anything. I love you but guess what, Jesus loves you more."

What a relief, it felt as though a ton of bricks had been lifted from my shoulders. I loved Virginia; I loved her with a passion, what a woman of God.

I once went to a seminar and heard the speaker say that in order for our relationships to work, we need to marry someone at the same level of our self esteem. How profound! Well, the biblical translation of that quote is, 'not to be unequally yoked with unbelievers.' I am blessed to have a partner who is truly devoted to the Lord.

As I turned off the ignition she continued talking, "Honey, this experience will bring us closer to the Lord and allow us to exercise faith. This journey will force us to let go and let God, and watch Him make a way where there is no way."

She eased off the door and I came out the car. I pulled her close to me and wrapped my arms around her, I felt safe and secure and prayed that God would keep us together until he was ready to take us home to be with Him. I bent down and whispered in her ear, "Sweetheart, after twenty five years, I'm still crazy about you. I love you Virginia, together we're going to beat this recession."

"I love you too Ray and with the help of the Lord we will, how about church on Sunday? We've missed a few Sundays because you had to be working on some projects for the job, but now there's nothing standing in the way."

"You bet, we will be in church on Sunday bright and early and I know Ryan and Rebecca will be happy to be in Sunday school also."

That night I tossed and turned while Virginia slept peacefully. I switched on the reading light and opened my Bible to Psalm 91. Talk about security–

Psalm 91, the secret place of security for God's children.

Abiding in the Shadow of the Almighty
1. He that dwelleth in the secret place of the

Most High shall abide under the shadow of the Almighty

2. I will say of the Lord, He is my refuge and my fortress: my God, in Him will I trust;

3. Surely, he will deliver thee from the snare of the fowler, and from the noisome pestilence.

4. He shall cover thee with feathers, and under his wings shalt thou trust: His truth shall be thy shield and buckler.

5. Thou shall not be afraid for the terror by night, nor for the arrow that flieth by day;

6. Nor for the pestilence that walketh in the darkness, nor for the destruction that wasteth at noonday.

7. A thousand shall fall at thy side, and ten thousand at thy right hand;, but It shall not come nigh thee.

8. Only with thine eyes shalt thou behold and see the reward of the wicked.

9. Because thou hast made the LORD,

which is my refuge, even the MOST High my habitation.

10. There shall no evil befall thee, neither shall any plague come nigh thy Dwelling.

11. For he shall gibe his angels charge over thee, Mt. 4.6 · Lk. 4.10

12. They shall bear thee up in their hands, lest thou dash they foot against a stone.
Mt. 4.6 · Lk. 4.11

13. Thos shalt tread upon the lion and adder: the young lion and the dragon shalt thou trample under feet. Lk. 10.19.

14. Because he hath set his love upon me, therefore will I deliver him: I will set him on high, because he hath known my name.

15. He shall call upon me, and I will answer him: I will be with him in trouble: I will deliver him and honor him.

16. With long life will I satisfy him, and show him my salvation.

Every verse in this Psalm is a promise of our Heavenly Father, to cover, shield and protect us. This is the kind of promise that stands forever, no wavering, God's word is truth. After reading that Psalm that morning I vowed to read it every day so I could meditate on it and write it on the tablets of my heart. I knew it would come in handy and be my weapon in time of need. I went back to bed and slept like a baby until the sun came up with my sweetheart curled up in my arms. My heart was still filled with joy as I shared verse after verse of this powerful Psalm with Virginia. It's funny how you often read the word and it sometimes takes years for it to come alive and truly bless your heart.

That Saturday felt somewhat different, maybe I was conscious that I was unemployed. Virginia helped me to reorganize my home office and incorporated some of the memoirs that I had brought home. That day I thought about JR and moved his card from the back of my pocket to my wallet, at this point I was not opposed to talking with him, I'd give it a week or two and if I didn't hear from him I'd certainly give him a call.

I had to make a concerted effort not to focus on the company, you'd think it was a part of my DNA, but I needed to purge myself of that and replace it with something that was more powerful, more lasting, like the blood of Jesus.

Chapter 4

Even though I walk through the
Valley of the shadow of death
Your perfect love is casting out fear
And even when I'm caught in the
Middle of the storms of this life
I won't turn back
I know you are near

And I will fear no evil
For my God is with me
And if my God is with me
Whom then shall I fear?
Whom then shall I fear?

Oh no, You never let go

Through the calm and through the storm

Oh no, You never let go

In every high and every low

Oh no, You never let go

Lord, You never let go of me

And I can see a light that is coming

For the heart that holds on

A glorious light beyond all compare

And there will be an end to these troubles

But until that day comes

We'll live to know You here on the earth

And I will fear no evil

For my God is with me

And if my God is with me

Whom then shall I fear?

Whom then shall I fear?

Oh no, You never let go

Through the calm and through the storm

Oh no, You never let go

In every high and every low

Oh no, You never let go

Lord, You never let go of me.

Matt Redman

This was the song I walked into with over 800 plus voices glorifying and praising God. The Holy Spirit took charge as I lifted my hands and worshipped the King of King's and Lord of Lord's. Three Sunday's ago when I came to church; I had the perfect life, with my big paying job! Now, a few weeks later I'm back in church, no job! I wonder how many people in the congregation were impacted by the recession. My company laid off 150 workers and other companies were laying off people also. There were so many people who were losing their homes; people were walking away from relationships; the suicide rate had increased and more people were dying of heart attacks;

people had lost a fortune in ponzi schemes that was masked as sound investments. We all needed a wake-up call. We were so consumed with the possibility of becoming rich that we didn't have much time for God. Now we needed Him more than ever before and this was the perfect song to reaffirm that God will not let us go; He will be there to carry us through the calm and through the storm.

That morning I decided that church was going to be a permanent staple in my life, so attending church was going to be a priority.

Pastor Danny was under the anointing that morning as he took the microphone and started to pray for individuals who were affected by the recession. I was in total shock as it seemed as though the picture in my brain was miraculously transmitted to his heart as he was praying about everything that had just gone through my mind.

"God is this how you work?" I asked quietly.

My heart was filled with happiness knowing that God cared. I wondered what the sermon would be about.

Pastor invited us to read along with him from the book of Daniel chapter 3. I knew the story quite well but had not read it recently.

Daniel Chapter 3: 1-30

The Deliverance from the Fiery Furnace

1. Nebuchadnez'zar the king made an image of gold, whose height was threescore cubits, and the breadth thereof six cubits: he set it up in the plain of Dura, in the province of Babylon.

2. Then Nebuchadnez'zar the king sent to gather together the princes, the governors, and the captains, the judges, the treasurers, the counselors, the sheriffs, and all the rulers of the provinces, to come to the dedication of the image which Nebuchadnez'zar the king had set up.

3. Then the princes, the governors, and captains, the judges, the treasurers, the counselors, the sheriffs, and all the rulers of the provinces, were gathered together unto the dedication of the image that Nebuchadnez'zar the king had set up; and they stood before the image that Nebuchadnez'zar had set up.

4. Then a herald cried aloud, To you it is commanded, O people, nations, and languages,

5. that at what time ye hear the sound of the cornet, flute, harp, sackbut, psaltery, dulcimer, and all kinds of music, ye fall down and worship the golden image that Nebuchadnez'zar the king hath set up:

6. and whoso falleth not down and

worshippeth shall the same hour be cast into the midst of a burning fiery furnace.

7. Therefore at that time, when all the people heard the sound of the cornet, flute, harp, sackbut, psaltery, and all kinds of music, all the people, the nations, and the languages, fell down and worshipped the golden image that Nebuchadnez'zar the king had set up.

8. ¶ Wherefore at that time certain Chalde'ans came near, and accused the Jews.

9. They spake and said to the king Nebuchadnez'zar, O king, live for ever.

10. Thou, O king, hast made a decree, that every man that shall hear the sound of the cornet, flute, harp, sackbut, psaltery, and dulcimer, and all kinds of music, shall fall down and worship the golden image:

11. and whoso falleth not down and worshippeth, that he should be cast into the midst of a burning fiery furnace.

12.   There are certain Jews whom thou hast set over the affairs of the province of Babylon, Shadrach, Meshach, and Abed'nego; these men, O king, have not regarded thee: they serve not thy gods, nor worship the golden image which thou hast set up.

13. ¶ Then Nebuchadnez'zar in his rage and fury commanded to bring Shadrach, Meshach, and Abed'nego. Then they brought these men before the king.

14. Nebuchadnez'zar spake and said unto them, Is it true, O Shadrach, Meshach, and Abed'nego? do not ye serve my gods, nor worship the golden image which I have set up?

15. Now if ye be ready that at what time ye hear the sound of the cornet, flute, harp, sackbut, psaltery, and dulcimer, and all kinds of music, ye fall down and worship the image which I have made; well: but if ye worship not, ye shall be cast the same hour into the midst of a burning fiery furnace; and who is that God that shall deliver you out of my hands?

16. ¶ Shadrach, Meshach, and Abed'nego, answered and said to the king, O Nebuchadnez'zar, we are not careful to answer thee in this matter.

17. If it be so, our God whom we serve is able to deliver us from the burning fiery furnace, and he will deliver us out of thine hand, O king.

18. But if not, be it known unto thee, O king, that we will not serve thy gods, nor worship the golden image which thou hast set up.

19. ¶ Then was Nebuchadnez'zar full of fury, and the form of his visage was changed against Shadrach, Meshach, and Abed'nego: therefore he spake, and commanded that they should heat the furnace one seven times more than it was wont to be heated.

20. And he commanded the most mighty men that were in his army to bind Shadrach, Meshach, and Abed'nego, and to cast them into the burning fiery furnace.

21. Then these men were bound in their coats, their hose, and their hats, and their other garments, and were cast into the midst of the burning fiery furnace.

22. Therefore because the king's commandment was urgent, and the furnace exceeding hot, the flame of the fire slew those men that took up Shadrach, Meshach, and Abed'nego.

23. And these three men, Shadrach, Meshach, and Abed'nego, fell down bound into the midst of the burning fiery furnace.

24. ¶ Then Nebuchadnez'zar the king was astonished, and rose up in haste, and

spake, and said unto his counselors, Did not we cast three men bound into the midst of the fire? They answered and said unto the king, True, O king.

25. He answered and said, Lo, I see four men loose, walking in the midst of the fire, and they have no hurt; and the form of the fourth is like the Son of God.

26. ¶ Then Nebuchadnez'zar came near to the mouth of the burning fiery furnace, and spake, and said, Shadrach, Meshach, and Abed'nego, ye servants of the most high God, come forth, and come hither. Then Shadrach, Meshach, and Abed'nego, came forth of the midst of the fire.

27. And the princes, governors, and captains, and the king's counselors, being gathered together, saw these men, upon whose bodies the fire had no power, nor was a hair of their head singed, neither were their coats changed, nor the smell of fire had passed on them.

28. Then Nebuchadnez'zar spake, and said, Blessed be the God of Shadrach, Meshach, and Abed'nego, who hath sent his angel, and delivered his servants that trusted in him, and have changed the king's word, and yielded their bodies, that they might not serve nor worship any god, except their own God.

29. Therefore I make a decree, That every people, nation, and language, which speak any thing amiss against the God of Shadrach, Meshach, and Abed'nego, shall be cut in pieces, and their houses shall be made a dunghill; because there is no other God that can deliver after this sort.

30. Then the king promoted Shadrach, Meshach, and Abed'nego, in the province of Babylon.

"What a mighty God we serve, the same God that

delivered Shadrach, Meshach and Abednego can deliver you from your fiery furnaces. What does that represent in your life? Is it a relationship that has gone sour, one of abuse, disrespect and infidelity? Or is it a massive layoff from the so-called job security. Maybe it's the foreclosure notice that was served to you this week, or the eviction notice demanding that you move in three days. Maybe you were part of the investment scams that promised high returns on investments, where millions lost their lives savings with zero return.

If you can believe in a broken system that has failed you time and time again, why not turn to God today and put your trust in the only secure system known to man? Let's put our trust in the only One with an unblemished record. Let's put our trust in the One who walked in the fire with his servants and not even the hair on their head was singed, nor did they even smell of smoke. Let's put our trust in the One who will carry us through our fiery furnace. No matter what you might be going through today, know that God has a bigger plan for your life. You might say Pastor, I just lost my job, well believe God that He has something better in store for you. Walt Disney started Disney in the great Depression of 1929. At that time, many people thought he was crazy but he was up against an economic slump that lasted for ten years. The longest and most severe depression ever experienced in North America and different parts of the world. Despite some banks being forced into insolvency and the collapse of the stock market, Walt Disney relentlessly pursued his dream. He disregarded the negative comments of his critics and naysayers, and succeeded in launching Disney during the great depression of 1929.

I believe this quote sums up Walt Disney's accomplishments; 'Your world is a living expression of how you are using and have used your mind.'

Romans 12:2

And be not conformed to this world: but be ye transformed by the renewing of your mind, that ye may prove what is that good, and acceptable, and perfect, will of God.

It is imperative that you stay clear of negativity, believe in God and believe in your ability to achieve whatever you put your mind to. There are two things standing between you and your goals; self doubt and the negative relationships in your life. You might have lost your job thinking that you were the head but you were in fact the tail, but God can re-instate you and make you the head. Stop limiting God; you could become the next Walt Disney.

Don't think that because you've lost your job the world is coming to an end, embrace the change and step out of your comfort zone. Like a world renown motivational speaker, Les Brown says it best, "When you do the things that are easy, life is hard but when you do the things that are hard, life is easy. This recession is not the first and it will not be the last, they come and go and they last for a season, the only thing that is lasting is salvation. But the God we serve is the God who makes the impossible possible. Let's take a look at;

Joshua 24:13
So I gave you a land on which you did not toil and cities you did not build; and you live in them and eat from vineyards and olive groves that you did not plant.

Proverbs 13:22
The wealth of the sinner is laid up for the just.

Just like how God made Shadrach, Meshach, and Abednego 'Fire-Proof' God can make you 'Recession-Proof', but you must first learn to trust him."

When pastor's sermon ended, I knew God used this sermon to renew my faith and trust in Him. He also removed the stigma about Network Marketing and I now understood where Virginia was coming from. I was even open to speaking with JR. All I know, I was not going to worry because God was going to deliver me and open a way that would bring glory and honor to His name.

On our way home Ryan shared the verse that he learnt in Sunday school.

Proverbs 3:5
Trust in the Lord with all thine heart; and lean not unto thine own understanding. In all thy ways acknowledge him and he will direct your path.

I found myself talking out aloud: 'Lord I got it, the song, the sermon and now little Ryan, you're precious and I love you."

"I love you too Daddy," little Rebecca chimed in. Everyone smiled. Turning to Rebecca I said, "I love you little princess," "And mommy loves you too," Virginia added, "And me too," Ryan said as he snuggled up next to her in the back seat. Rebecca was beaming. Wow, what love!

Chapter 5

It was Monday morning, and it was the first time in twenty-five years that my wife was leaving for work with me staying at home. Then I thought about the Walt Disney story that Pastor Danny shared in church. Virginia and I had devotion before she left, and she just blessed my heart and made me feel so valued. What a jewel! I ironed her clothes as she showered and I made her breakfast while she got dressed. We were not going to go apart because I lost my job; I was not going to blame her because the real estate market crashed and we bought that house primarily because she loved it. We would be like our good friends Desmond and Catherine Malcolm, who secured their marriage despite the massive loss in personal and business assets. Like them, we were going to quickly bolt up our back doors so our love of twenty-five years would not escape. With the help of God we were going to work through this together and like the three men of God who were fire-proof our relationship was officially recession- proof.

I kissed my sweetheart goodbye and went to the kitchen to put the orange juice back in the fridge, when Ena, the children's nanny walked in. "Good morning Mr. Ray, you're not feeling well today, sir?"

"No, I'm fine Ena," I answered.

"It's just that I've never seen you stay home from work before, sir."

I almost wished she hadn't asked.

"Ena, I'm no longer with that company, I was laid off on Friday."

"I'm sorry to hear that sir, but does that mean I'm going to lose my job?"

"We don't plan on laying you off anytime soon Ena, but we're trusting the Lord to open a way for me. We'll keep you posted, but no need to worry when you can pray.

Ryan and Rebecca ran in the kitchen and embraced me, Ryan seemed puzzled but didn't ask any questions. After they ate breakfast Ena took Ryan to school and Rebecca to the library for her, 'Once upon a time,' session.

The place was finally quiet and I just started to praise the Lord. I was so deep in worship that I almost did not hear the phone ringing. I picked it up and there was a familiar voice on the other end, but I didn't readily recognize it.

"Mr. Gordon, good morning, it's JR. Sorry to hear you got laid off last Friday sir, that was a terrible thing for Mr. Sinclair to have done, he had you layoff 145 people then turned around and terminated you."

"JR, its ok, what I've learned in the past two days is maybe more than I've learned in the 25 years with the company. But do me a favor, we're no longer in Corporate America so let's drop the formalities, Ray is fine, and JR is still ok?"

"Sure, I'm cool with that," JR replied and then he continued, "Well I assume you have not heard the news, sir."

"What news?" I asked.

"Mr. Sinclair died at about 5:30 this morning from

a massive heart attack, by the time he arrived at the hospital he was pronounced dead."

I was dumbstruck, couldn't utter a word. "Are you there sir," JR asked.

"Yes, JR."

He paused for a moment then said, "Is it ok for me to say something that has been on my mind sir?"

What's that?" I asked.

"Mr. Gordon, you know you were the one running the company, everyone in the department knew that. Mr. Sinclair died from FEAR, fear of running a company when he had no idea what to do. Can you imagine the tension he had over the past two days? He chose to die rather than face his mountain. I feel pity for him and I wished he hadn't done that."

I was still lost for words and as I listened to JR my mind recapped my last meeting with Mr. Sinclair, he seemed totally detached from everything. I never understood his lack of response to the proposal to reorganize the company. In retrospect, I think he had already given up from Friday. I quietly sent a prayer up for his wife, Paula and their two boys.

JR interrupted my train of thoughts, "Mr. Gordon, I believe once Mr. Sinclair realized that they were not going to keep you, he gave up, accepted defeat and threw in the towel from then."

Just then, the call-waiting signal on my phone beeped. In order to take the incoming call I hurriedly requested, "Excuse me a moment JR, please don't hang up let me catch this call."

"Hello," the voice sounded distant, somewhat of an Asian accent.

"May I please speak to Mr. Ray Gordon, the female caller requested.

"Speaking," I answered. Kindly hold for Mr. Kobayashi, the owner of IT Enterprises.

"Maam, could he possibly call back in an hour, I'm currently on a business call." I said.

"Sir, he's very busy and is about to make you an offer you will not be able to refuse."

"I would appreciate if Mr. Kobayashi could call back in an hour. Thank you."

I was determined not to have them jerk my chain again, I was going to be in control this time around. In total bewilderment I clicked over to continue my conversation with JR.

So I felt like acting goofy and threw a question at

JR "So what do you think I should do about Mr. Kobayashi's offer?"

I felt stupid and wanted to take back the question as JR had no idea what transpired on the other line. "Well did you have a chance to speak with Mr. Kobayashi, Sir?"

He was asking as though he knew who Mr. Kobayashi was. So in a puzzled voice I answered no.

"Mr. Gordon, while you were on the other line the Holy Spirit showed me that you were going to get an offer from the owner of IT Enterprises and that you should not say yes or no at this moment. Tell them you need some time to pray on it."

My mouth was to the floor for more reasons than one, I didn't know that JR was a believer so I knew God was in this. The reason I knew God was in this was because the Holy Spirit told me not to speak with Mr. Kobayashi at this moment, but to tell him to call back in an hour so I could get back on the phone with JR.

"Mr. Gordon, God has some big things in store for you, the Lord is not speaking through me right now, this is from me, JR. If you ever decided to go back to IT Enterprises, please let it be on your terms, meaning God's terms. Take a few weeks off and start your own business before you re-start theirs. They need you desperately because you've successfully run the company for the past eight years. Ask God's guidance in directing you to the right home base business and work it along side your job, so if you're ever let go again, you'll welcome the change as it should not alter your financial stability."

"JR, please call me Ray, now that I know we are brothers in Christ, I'm going to trust you to introduce me to the world of Network Marketing and study the lives of the folks who've been successful in it. But you know JR, I have promised the Lord that I'm going to pray about everything before I make a move, that way there'll be no regrets. Hey, speaking of praying, I need to hear from the Lord before Mr. Kobayashi calls back."

"Go take care of business, we'll talk later, I will be praying for you too," JR said…

"JR remember Mrs. Sinclair and the boys in your prayers please." I pleaded.

As I got up from my knees the phone rang, it was exactly an hour since I hung up from Japan.
I picked up the receiver, "Hello,"

"Mr. Ray Gordon please,"

I smiled as the accent gave my name a different pronunciation.

"Speaking," I answered.

"Please hold for Mr. Kobayashi."

"Certainly," I replied.

"Mr. Gordon, I always felt I should have been speaking with you over the past eight years instead of Mr. Sinclair, sorry he had to die in order for us to speak. I would like you to take over as CEO of IT Enterprises, effective immediately, so you can spearhead the company through this transitional period. With one hundred and forty-nine less employees it's going to take extreme focus and a no nonsense approach to keep our company in the black and make it very profitable. You are the only man for this job Mr. Gordon and I am willing to compensate you accordingly.

I know you were given a severance package with six months' salary, I propose that you keep the salary, in addition I'll bring you back with an annual salary of $250,000, 100 percent company contribution for health and a $1 million life insurance policy, plus car allowance is also included.

I don't know if you have someone in mind who you'd want to be your VP, but if not, you can hire from outside and bring in a good candidate with a starting salary of $125,000 annually.

How soon can you get to the office Mr. Gordon? I need for you to start right away."

"Mr. Kobayashi, your offer is very generous and I thank you for entrusting me with such great responsibilities, however, I am going to need some time to pray on this offer before accepting it. In addition, I'd like to play a part in helping to put away Mr. Sinclair respectfully before assuming his position. Would it be okay to have further communication with you a week from today?"

"Did I hear you say pray? That's unbelievable! Mr. Gordon, if I don't have a definite answer from you a week from today, I will fly someone in from Japan and have them run the company efficiently and profitably," Mr. Kobayashi replied.

"I understand, have a good day sir."

Chapter 6

'Is this what happens when we implicitly trust you Lord?'

How I wish I could reach out to my family and friends and tell them about the awesomeness of the God we serve, and what happens when we trust Him wholeheartedly. We limit God when we doubt him. He will not reward doubt, fear and faithlessness, so why do we spend so much time with such negative emotions. Immediately the Holy Spirit warmed my heart and reminded me of God's promise:

Deuteronomy 28:2

And all these blessings shall come on thee, and overtake thee, if thou shalt hearken unto the voice of the Lord thy God.

"Overtake me Lord? Am I to understand that when I serve and obey you, your blessings are going to come after me, and overtake me even though I don't deserve it?

God this is what I'm experiencing right now: I have worked for this company for twenty-five years, managed it for the past eight years, I have been laid off for three days and was almost to the point where I became angry with you. But I came to my senses and I totally let go and trusted you one hundred percent. And Father, in less than twenty-five hours after getting to that place in my walk with you, your blessings have overtaken me.

Instead of losing my job I'm being asked to return

to the company, assuming the highest position, instead of the six months pay that I thought was an insult, after serving a company for almost half my life, I get to keep the severance package plus receive a $50,000 annual increase. One hundred percent paid contribution to my family's health insurance plan, $1 million in life insurance and car allowance, which is an additional $15,000 per year.

Lord, why do we hesitate to serve you and miss out on your blessings, which is F-R-E-E! Absolutely Free, yet, we choose a harder life because of disobedience and lack of faith. Help us not to complicate matters, let's keep it simple and live for you, serve you, obey you and experience your goodness forever! A reminder from the Holy Spirit;

Proverbs 10:22
The blessing of the LORD, it maketh rich, and he addeth no sorrow with it."

Though this was an attractive offer, I was going to seek the Lord and ask him to confirm that this is what he wanted for me at this time in my life.

That evening when Virginia came home from work, I eagerly shared the day's happenings with her. She would occasionally burst out, "Hallelujah, thank you Jesus."

Virginia was in tune with the Holy Spirit and after I laid it all out she held my hands, closed her eyes and prayed. As I stood there waiting on the Lord, my wife prophetically spoke;

"I have heard your cry and have seen the yearning in your heart to serve me. You thirst after me and give me praises all the day long. Your worries I have turned into trust and your fear into faith. I have called you by your name and I will bless you, from the far corners of the earth will they give unto you. I will re-establish you and you will be the head and not the tail. Join forces with JR and work side by side with him as you return to this assignment. Continue to praise me and just as how I have blessed you, I want you to give back unsparingly to my work."

My eyes were teary, but this time it was tears of joy. My heart was overwhelmed because God was confirming his love for me. Wow, my wife, had a direct line to God; this was the confirmation I needed. Thank you Lord!

I did not hear back from JR that day but early the following morning he was the first caller. He was such a positive, vibrant individual, it's funny how God has a way of bringing people in our lives when we least expect. I took the opportunity to invite JR over, so we could have a chance to talk about the goodness of the Lord over coffee and get to know each other. I could sense the benefits of this relationship, but how often do we stay in negative relationships that drain us and leave us feeling hopeless? Negative relationships tear down while positive relationships build-up.

Proverbs 18:21
Death and life are in the power of the tongue: and they that love it shall eat the fruit thereof.

JR was at the door in less than 45 minutes, and for the first time I was seeing him outside the corporate setting. You could see the goodness of the Lord in him and his spirit was lively and vigorous.

"Good morning Mr. Gordon," he said enthusiastically.

"Ok JR, stop right there, we're finally going to get this right, once and for all. You're in my home, right?" JR nodded, "it's Ray, Ray, Ray, Ray, Ray, got it? We're brothers in Christ; we don't say Mr. Jesus or Mr. God."

JR chuckled, "Ok Ray, I got it!"

JR followed me to the breakfast nook where we sat together and had coffee and toast. He was curious to know how the conversation went with Mr. Kobayashi.

"JR, you were right on the money. He offered me much more than I ever expected, but I respectfully told him that I had to pray about it. JR, this experience with Mr. Kobayashi was God's way of demonstrating his undiluted love for me. I don't know any other way to put it, because if I was responsible to put a re-hiring package together, it wouldn't be anything close to what was offered to me. Of course, God used Virginia to confirm that I should take the offer but the Lord also showed her that I should join forces with you and work side by side as I get ready to return to my assignment."

JR listened in silence, then turning to me he said, "God is showing me to share my story with you."

"Wow, would love to hear it…" I responded.

"I was raised in a home where there was a lot of turmoil, and as early as four I would go next door to play with my friend Brandon as he had loving parents. When I was seven years old my parents divorced, my father didn't want to have the responsibility of raising me and my mother wanted to go to nursing school. She had to make a choice between staying home with me or sending me to live with my grandparents.

Living with my grandparents was probably the best thing that ever happened to me, they were kind, giving and loved me unconditionally. Years later when my mother returned to take me to live with her I refused to leave grandma and grandpa. When I was eleven I gave my heart to the Lord and was baptized shortly after. I attended the University of Florida and graduated with a degree in Computer Science. I fell in love with someone I met while in college and she became pregnant with our baby prior to getting married. We had a courthouse wedding as we didn't have the money to do it big. I found a job in the IT department of one of the local universities while my wife had a thriving home based business called, 'Storybook Wedding,' she did the consulting and sourced everything that was required for a wedding from beginning to end. She loved her business and was the best at it. She was the one who made me understand the value of having a home based business; there are so many perks. Once you get started, please speak with your tax advisor and he will highlight the benefits.

Anyway, one weekend there was a big football game at the University of Florida and a group of guys from the Alumni were driving up together. My wife was not able to come as one of her events was scheduled for that weekend also. About an hour into the journey, I started to experience severe stomach cramps, it got so bad that I had to pull off the highway to use a bathroom at a nearby restaurant. After being washed with cold sweat and goose bumps I reluctantly decided to forego the game and return home.

There was an unfamiliar car in my drive way. I did not open the garage but slowly opened the front door. The aroma of freshly cut lily's and a sweet fragrance from candles welcomed me. My insecurities surfaced as I opened my daughter's door and discovered that she was not there. I shuddered as I opened my bedroom door and caught my wife in adultery. The stranger's car left in minutes while I wrestled with a sea of unanswered questions. Disgust, disappointment, distrust and anger confronted me all at once and I asked God why. A few hours went by and my wife approached me with her head bent low, "I have something I need to say to you."

I did not answer. She continued to talk to me. 'I

know you believe you are Susie's dad, but you are not, I can't hide it from you anymore. Her father just left. I'm sorry for lying to you all these years, but I must move on with my life.'

Ray what is really ironic about all of this, a week before this incident one of our neighbor's had just lost his job and his wife was so sick and tired of all the stuff that was going wrong that she asked him to leave. Well one evening I saw him outside walking back to the house with the mail. He looked really distraught and I couldn't help but notice. He told me that he had recently lost his job, they had just been served with the foreclosure notice and his wife wanted a divorce.

Well I stopped dead in my tracks and saw where my wife and I could help save their marriage. Later that day they both came by, and I took John, and my wife took Kathy. After, a few hours we came together and prayed. God intervened and John went back home and unpacked. I told them that in a relationship, there's no such thing as fifty/fifty, its one hundred percent all the way and God has to be in the center of it all, otherwise it's not going to work.

John and Kathy had two extra bedrooms, so they decided to sign up for two foster children and were approved. The earning from the foster care was able to replace John's income.

My immediate reaction, when I contemplated this, was I just saved my neighbor's marriage and now I'm losing mine. It was not easy, but though they're different situations, like you, this experience has solidified my relationship with the Lord.

It doesn't matter what we're going through. There may be dozens of reasons why we can justify feeling down and out and why we should possibly throw in the towel, but there are so many more reasons why we should turn to the Lord and renew our faith in Him. If he cares for the sparrows and the lilies, don't you think he cares far more for us, who are made in his image and likeness?

Here is the scripture the Holy Spirit used to comfort me:

Deuteronomy 31:6
Be strong and of a good courage, fear not, nor be afraid of them: for the Lord thy God, he it is that doth go with thee; he will not fail thee, nor forsake thee.

Psalms 118:8
It is better to trust in the Lord than to put confidence in man.

I'm just getting back on my feet but I'm going to be ok. I'm taking this journey called life, with God as my pilot, and I'm not trying to rush into anything or get ahead of God. He is the Creator; He has the hand book for my life so He's the only one who can fix me as I know I'm a work in progress. As for my wife, I could only have forgiven her with the help of God, of which I'm reminded constantly;

Psalm 66:18

If I regard iniquity in my heart the Lord will not hear me.

"JR, I would never have known in a million years that you've gone through anything like this, your confidence and boldness is infectious. May the Almighty God shower you with his love and may he set you separate and apart, so you may be a beacon of light to millions. Lord if there is any little residue of unforgiveness, please flush it out and give JR a new heart, one that panteth after you." With his head bowed, he just kept saying, "Thank you Lord, thank you!"

"JR, would you have an interest in becoming, VP of

IT Enterprises?" I asked.

"Ray the old JR would have been bouncing off the wall and saying yes to the offer. But I'm a lot mellower today. The Lord has helped me launch my Network Marketing business about a year ago and I promised Him that I was going to help thousands of people who have lost their jobs and lost their vision. I am reminded of;

Proverbs 29:18
Where there is no vision, the people perish: but he that keeps the law, happy is he.

"JR, that is commendable, I appreciate your commitment to help others succeed and know that God will bless you. I'm totally green about Network Marketing, what can you tell me about it?"
"Ray, I might not have all the answers but over the past 12 months, I have learned quite a bit. Please stop me if you have any questions so I can address

it. So let me explain.

"Network Marketing, is a legitimate business model that is rapidly dominating the way business is done in the 21st century. In the United States over 14 million people are actively involved in Network Marketing and globally, approximately 100 million.

A Network Marketing organization spends time and money and legally establishes themselves in the market place. The idea is for those organizations to recruit individuals to market their products and services for a minimal investment. Once you are a representative of the organization, you can then bring others on board at which time they are given the same exact opportunity. Once you build what is referred to as a 'down line,' you become qualified to earn residual income from their efforts.

This could start out very small, but because many

folks have a 'get rich quick' mentality, they fall out early in the game, giving a bad name to the industry.

There is nothing quick about building a solid Network Marketing business. It could take as little as six months for the very aggressive and driven individuals, or as long as ten years. It's a personalized business; you get out of it what you put into it.

Network Marketing is also known as multi-level marketing (MLM), for a company that is required to be licensed and registered with various governmental bodies, it is impossible for it to be a pyramid or a scam. Due to the negativity that surrounds Network Marketing, a web site has been constructed to protect the good businesses and expose the bad ones. Feel free to look up: www. mlmia.com

Here is the one reason why most people fail at Network Marketing. They have no clue on how to successfully build a home based business from the ground up. Check out this site, it will Point, Guide and Direct you to information that could make you a star in the Network Marketing Industry. www.pgdnews.com

The three main reasons why Network Marketing is a good choice;

Residual income - you are paid on what you do and also from the efforts of all the people who fall in your down line (most of which you might not even know).

Leveraging - I believe J. Paul Getty, gives a great definition of leveraging: 'I would rather make one percent on the efforts of one hundred people than one hundred percent on my own efforts.' If you only worked your business five hours per week but you had a down line of one hundred people each working five hours, therefore you would be getting paid on five hundred and five hours instead of five. This is the power of Network Marketing vs a regular job.

Duplication – Also known as geometric growth. You duplicate yourself in one and as that concept continues you could end up with hundreds or possibly thousands in your down line. Keep in mind that it only started with you.

Network Marketing is a 'peoples business.' It does not require a college education or a certain color or height, it's a level playing field and to win in this industry, you need to be driven, determined and have a burning desire to succeed.

The only guarantee that comes with Network Marketing is; training and support. Remember if you don't succeed, I don't succeed, so it's in my best interest to help you achieve your goals. However, if you like guarantees, you decide at what level you want to get in, how much time you can put in, how many people you want to help and how much money you want to make. You hold the keys to your future.

The recession is a great time for entrepreneurs, there is no better time to start a home-based business. Ray, did you know that there were 14 big businesses that started during the recession of the 50's and 70's? Let me just take a minute and mention six of them.

Hyatt Corp: Started during the recession of 1957-1958. Today they operate more than 365 hotels in 25 countries.

Burger King Corp: Recession start-up. Company began in 1954 and opened its Miami store during the 1957 recession. Successful signature burger

—the Whopper. Company operates more than 11,100 locations in 65 countries.

The Jim Henson Company: Began in 1958 recession by famous puppeteer Jim Henson. It is responsible for some of the best-known puppet characters such as; Elmo, Miss Piggy, and Kermit the Frog.

IHOP Corp: Recession start-up. Company began 1958 by owners, Al and Jerry Lapin. Franchising was a hit. There are more than 1,300 locations across the U.S.

FedEx Corp: Began operations in 1973 as Federal Express. Founder Frederick W. Smith now manages more than 7.5 million shipments everyday worldwide.

Microsoft Corp. Started in the 1975 recession, by Harvard University dropout Bill Gates. Today, the company is estimated to earn more than $60 billion in revenue per year.

It has been proven that more millionaires are made during a recession, because people are forced to be more creative and tap into their God given talent. Ray, you might be green to Network Marketing but you're so experienced in other areas, I know I can learn from you, but you couldn't have chosen a better time to start."

I had listened earnestly to JR and was beside myself with the information he had provided me, "How come no one had the courage to share this information with me all these years. I am so happy I took the time to listen. Not to mention the weight loss products. Virginia will be elated with this line of products. She's serious about staying forever young and maintaining her ideal weight, so yeah, we'll pray about it, and I will have an answer for you before I go back to IT."

"Sounds good to me Ray. Thanks again for giving me the opportunity to share."

Chapter 7

"Honey, I was talking with JR this morning and do you know they had to hold Mr. Sinclair's body a couple days at the hospital as there was no room at the morgue."

"That is crazy," Virginia said, and then continued, "I can't believe what I'm hearing. I was just speaking with one of the girl's at the office and they were at a party on Saturday night and everyone was having a great time, when one of the guys got up and had to leave in the height of the celebration. When they inquired what the hurry was, he informed them that he was a funeral director and he'd not seen business this good in years. Everyone was astounded"

"Honey, stress is playing a major role in all of this. If folks would just take the Lord at his word and quit trying to solve all these problems on their own, life would be a lot less stressful.

Virginia, this scripture comes to mind;

1 Peter 5:7
Casting all your care upon him; for he careth for you.

After doing a bit of research on stress and heart attack this is what I found.

'The stress response is the body's way of pro-tecting us. Stress can help us stay alert, energetic and motivated, stress can literally save us. When we're driving and we suddenly hit on the brakes to avoid an accident, that's good stress. When we're exposed to stress long term it can cause serious health problems; for example, a heart attack and/or stroke, which could eventually claim our lives. Chronic stress can seriously diminish our ability to enjoy life, accomplish our goals, and maintain a healthy lifestyle.

It is advised that if you find that you're feeling stressed you need to change your diet and start practicing healthy eating habits. You need to maintain an alkaline diet, sixty percent alkaline foods and forty percent acid foods. The human blood ph should be 7.35-7.45

It is also recommend that you walk every day. Walking can protect the heart and circulatory system and even keep your weight down.

Supplement your diet with essential fatty acids, most of the food we're eating does not have all the nutrients and minerals we need, Omega 3 and

Omega 6 are vital for good health. Also eat lots of fruits and vegetables.

Oxygen; hydration and rest are also vital for a healthy lifestyle.

Since as far back as 1899 one of the best medicines that can help prevent a heart attack, increase the chance of survival during a heart attack, and reduce the risk of a second heart attack is Aspirin.

Heart attacks are caused by clogged arteries. Arteries get clogged when plaque builds up on artery walls, caused by too much fat and LDL cholesterol in the bloodstream.

Aspirin prevents heart attacks by keeping blood clots from forming. People should consult with their doctor about starting a daily aspirin regimen, or find out if they should avoid the use of aspirin."

Author's note: We know that there is a place for doctors in our society and we do not refute that, therefore the information shared is linked to both stress and heart attack as it relates to the story line. Please seek the advice of your health care professional before the implementation of any advice in this book.

Chapter 8

"Can't believe the week had flown by so quickly; thank God Mr. Sinclair was respectfully laid to rest, I pray that at some point in his life he accepted you Lord. I am drawn to

Matthew 16: 26

For what is a man profited, if he shall gain the whole world, and lose his own soul? Or what shall a man give in exchange for his soul?

Nothing!" It's funny how we work years to collect stuff that we protect with our lives, that no one else is allowed to touch. We get consumed with the cares of this world and have these collections become a part of someone else's collection when we go. Yet we spend so much time, effort and emotions into things that have no eternal value.

Matthew 6:19-21

"Lay not up for yourselves treasures upon earth, where moth and rust doth corrupt, and where thieves break through and steal. But lay up for yourselves treasures in heaven, where neither moth nor rust doth corrupt, and where thieves do not break through nor steal. For where your treasure is, there will your heart be also."

So where is your treasure? May God help us to re-prioritize our lives and put Him first.

Matthew 6:33...

"Seek ye first the kingdom of God, and his righteousness; and all these things shall be added unto you."

'How powerful are your promises Lord? Less than two weeks ago it seemed as though my life had ended and I thought for a moment that you had abandoned me. The only job that I had was taken from me and after my company terminated one hundred and forty-five employees, I too, was let go. At times I felt like flying into your face and confronting you, but before that thought even had a chance to settle, the Holy Spirit comforted me. And by the time I left church I gave everything completely over to you.'

You see it's easy to serve the Lord when things are going good, but I'm encouraging you to serve him even more when things are going bad. That's when your faith is truly tested, if you trust him then the rewards will be so much greater.

I encourage you to call on the Lord when you need him, he's available all the time, 24/7, you won't be disturbing him, even though he has billions of calls coming in at the same time, there's never a busy signal. Every call is personalized, write his number down and make sure you never lose it; call him every day he will never get tired of hearing from you.

Jeremiah 33:3...
Call to me, and I will answer you, and show you great and mighty things, which you know not.

Psalm 55:17...
Evening, and morning, and at noon, will I pray, and cry aloud: and he shall hear my voice.

I am not minimizing what you might be going through at this time; whatever it is I encourage you to seek the Lord's face and pray. It is evident that we are in spiritual warfare, so none of us are exempt from the attack of the enemy. But God has made preparation for us to overcome and be victorious. This is confirmed in;

Ephesians 6:12…

For we wrestle not against flesh and blood, but against principalities, against powers, against the rulers of the darkness of this world, against spiritual wickedness in high places.

Yes, we are in battle, but we're not alone, the angels of God have been assigned to us,

Psalm 91: 11 – 12…

For He shall give His angels charge over you, To keep you in all your ways.

In their hands they shall bear you up, Lest you dash your foot against a stone.

God has equipped us. Prayer is our weapon, and the word of God our sword, and with the angels of God encamping around us we cannot be defeated."

Wow, it was so good spending quality time with the Lord and just talking to him and waiting to hear from him. As I got ready to wrap up my private session with the Lord the door bell rang. I quickly went to open the door, and saw it was JR.

"So good to see you my brother," we embraced as we walked to the breakfast nook. This time the table was set, and I had prepared breakfast sandwiches for both of us. The glasses were filled with freshly squeezed orange juice and each setting had a bowl of fresh fruits.

With a smile JR turned to me, "You did all this man. I am really impressed!"

"Remember, I can do all things through Christ who strengthens me including preparing a gourmet meal from beginning to end."

With a chuckle JR replied, "Let me know more

about that gourmet meal I'd like to be around for tasting."

"Will keep you posted," I replied.

After breakfast I cleared the table and got ready for our meeting. When I was settled, I said to JR:

"You see JR I have given a lot of thought regarding our meeting and have done further research on the natural weight loss line. I had a detailed discussion with Virginia and as you know we pray about everything. We got the go-ahead this morning and we're ready to get involved. Also remember that I resume work on Monday and Virginia has a full time job. We're willing to learn the business, but based on our schedule we might only be able to consistently put in five hours per week, but with that commitment my long term goal is to be compensated for five hundred and five hours, but personally putting in only five hours. So go ahead and sign us up for the premier package. Virginia has already started making her list and will call you to confirm the date for our first meeting."

"Ray, you're a good student, I see you're a friend of J. Paul Getty, he's a friend of mine also." He chuckled as he spoke. "But I'm really excited that you and Virginia have decided to give Network Marketing a try, furthermore you're doing this with me. I promise that I will never let you down and I will lead with integrity and passion. Let's go ahead and set up your website, Your site will list all the benefits of the Natural Weight Loss Product. *Lower Cholesterol, *Increase Energy, *Reduce Appetite and Cravings, *Drastically helps Diabetics *Improves Bowel Function, *LowerTriglycerides, * All Natural – No Side Effects. Folks can join the business or purchase products online, here is your website information: www.loseitandfitit.com "JR, I would never have imagined that I would ever be involved in Network Marketing, but when you're obedient to the Lord He will remove the barriers and set the stage and all we have to do is to show up. JR, you are now our coach and mentor in this journey of Network Marketing, so now we're ready to follow your lead."

"Ray, I've got my work cut out for me, I'll be flying out to Atlanta tomorrow to get the business started there and then to New York and New Jersey for launchings also. Remember, if you need me to do three way calls I will make myself available, don't forget to edify me as an expert in the industry and I'll do the rest."

"JR, are you confident you can make a living from this Network Marketing business?"

"Ray this might not seem like a lot to you but remember that I've been doing this business part-time steadily, for a little more than a year. I'm not really in the habit of showing checks, but I just got this in the mail yesterday. It's a good thing I didn't go to the bank before coming here. But I know seeing is believing as the potential for earning is limitless."

JR showed me a check for $7,450!

He continued, "At the rate I'm going I should be able to triple this in three to six months. But don't get me wrong this is not the earning of the average person in Network Marketing. I'd like to think that there's nothing average about me, whatever I do I give it my all."

"So Network Marketing really works, eh. I had no idea that you could make this type of money. JR, I am so happy for you. Now I know why you didn't take me up on my offer. If you work it the way you plan to, in another year you'll be earning way more than what I'll be making at the job."

"That might be true Ray, but believe it or not, my first check was only $26.42 and it has increased every month since. The difference between Network Marketing and working in a corporate environment is, you don't have to wait to get an annual evaluation to receive an increase. You can choose to give yourself an increase every month, but believe me when I tell you, it's not easy, it's hard! Only the strong survive in Network Marketing. There's a handful of folks who make it BIG! Yet there are millions who're satisfied with maybe an extra $300.00 more per month. I was on a conference call the other day and learned that if the average household would bring home an extra $300 per month that would be enough to avoid foreclosure. So for you and I, that might just be a drop in the bucket, but for many families that's a significant amount."

"JR, anything that will contribute to the well being of the society will get my attention. Now I will be an advocate for Network Marketing and show individuals how they can make an extra $300 to $3,000 or $30,000 per month. All those single parents who're heads of household now have an opportunity to make a decent living. From what I'm learning from you, they need to be coachable, and they need to put the same level of commitment into this as they would their regular job. Little effort --- little pay, much effort ---- much pay!!!

"If it is to be, it's up to me, and it's also up to you."

Chapter 9

It was exactly one week since I had spoken with Mr. Kobayashi. I prayed before dialing the number and I felt quite at peace, knowing that the job was still there and that no one had been flown in from Japan to take over the running of the company. When I called, his assistant put me through immediately.

"Mr. Kobayashi, this is Ray Gordon, just calling to find out when would you like me to report to work?"

He chuckled, "Now is perfect. Good decision Mr. Gordon. There's really not much we need to talk about as you're just assuming your rightful position, especially since you have been running the company for the past eight years. Please be at the office by noon today. Everyone will report to you and you will report directly to me. By the time you arrive at the office the entire staff would have received the memo and everyone will know there is a new sheriff in town. Mr. Gordon, congratulations on your promotion to CEO of IT Enterprises. I am confident that under your leadership the success of the company will continue despite the economic downturn."

"Thank you Mr. Kobayashi."

For the first time, I felt empowered going back to a job where I was going to be paid well, but more importantly, knowing that JR, Virginia and I were building our home based business side by side with my corporate job.

I wish more people in America got it, it's called a Plan B, if you're laid off and you don't have an alternate plan to continue earning, of course you're going to get stressed and you're also going to get all the relevant issues that comes along with it. You can never have a positive outcome when you're unprepared. But when you have a back-up plan, you can make a smooth transition and keep living and maintaining the lifestyle that you're accustomed to.

If you're totally against Network Marketing, start a home based business right from your home, there are close to 500 different home based businesses to choose from, listed at the back of this book. You could start off with a little daycare business; you never know where that could take you. I recently met a lady who started a daycare in her basement twenty-five years ago, well, today she's a giant business woman, owns millions of dollars in Real Estate, all free and clear. Stop limiting God and put your creativity to work for you!

What is that idea that could take your life to the next level? I promise that whatever you do will not be easy, but it will be worth it. Like a few popular quotes, "You have to bear the cross before you can wear the crown, in other words, 'Nothing good comes easy,' in other words, 'No pain no gain,' in other words, 'every journey begins with the first step. So that's life, you cannot sit back and expect things to happen, you've got to get out of your comfort zone, trust God, and start the ball rolling.'

I hope one of these businesses will work for you, it doesn't matter which one, pull it out of your system, face it head on and pray about it. Once you get the okay from the Lord, put things into action and start to work it.

Don't let the fear of being laid off cripple you;

work on your Plan B, so you won't have to alter your lifestyle.

Are you living in Fear of losing your house?

Don't move out. Take care of your property, stay there for as long as you can and save your monthly payments to move out in case you are forced to.

Has your spouse walked out on you and blamed you for everything lost during the recession?

Hold your head high and know that if he or she is quick to leave now, it would be just a matter of time before he or she leaves anyway. Many partners are using the recession as an excuse to get out of their relationships. That's not the type of partner you want to be with. Stop searching for a mate; leave it to God and let Him find the next partner for you. Remember, make sure that you are not unequally yoked.

Let me ask you this question; If you knew for certain that today was your last day on earth, how would you live today?

Live your life with urgency; don't wait until you get sick to make God a priority, make him a priority today. If you have never invited the Lord Jesus into your life, make him Lord of your life today and secure your Salvation for Eternity. Always remember that this recession won't last but Salvation will.

If you would like to invite the Lord Jesus into your heart, please join me by saying this prayer:

Lord Jesus, I invite you to come into my heart today, please take away all my sins and worries and renew my faith in you. Please help me to be recession-proof. Your word says: That if I confess with my mouth, and believe in my heart that God raised Jesus from the dead, I will be saved. Lord I believe!

Having said the prayer you are now born into the family of God!

Romans 10:10...

For with the heart man believeth unto righteousness; and with the mouth confession is made unto salvation.

The word of God says: "Faith without works is dead," So if you are one of the millions, who are currently unemployed, here is a list of Home Based Businesses that will stimulate your creativity and awaken the giant inside you. Whatever that is, let's bring it out and start to fuel the economy:

Ecclesiastes 9:10

Whatsoever thy hand findeth to do, do it with thy might; for there is no work, nor device, nor knowledge, nor wisdom, in the grave, whither thou goest.

Home Based Businesses

(A)

Accountant

Adventure Tourism

Advertising Agency

Advertising Copywriter

Advertising Maps

Advertising Sheets

Advertising Specialty Sales

Aerobics Classes

Amusement Rides, Inflatable

Animal Behavior Consultant

Answering Service

Antifreeze Recycling Services

Antique and Collectibles Dealer

Antique Book and Magazine Dealer

Apartment Locator

Apiary

Appliance Repair

Architect

Art Consultant

Art Gallery

Artist, Feelance

Artist Management

Art Restoration

Association Management Service

Astrological Charts

Attorney

Author

Auto Sales

(B)

Baby Handprint and Fooprint Bronzing
   Service

Baby Proofing Service

Baby Shoe Bronzing Service

Balloon Animals

Balloon Decorating

Balloon Rides

Basketball Tournaments

Baskets, Specialty

Beautician

Beauty Consultant

Bed and Breakfast

Bicycle Repair

Bill Auditing Service

Billiards, Amateur League

Blind Cleaning

Bookkeeping Service

Braille Transcribing

Building/Home Inspection Service

Bulletin Board Advertising Service

Bumper Stickers

Business Broker

Business Consultant

Business Financing Service

Business Network Organizer

Business Plan Consultant

Business Plan Writer

Buttons/Badges

(C)

Cabinet Making

Cable TV Spots

Cake Decorating

Calligraphy

Candle Making

Canning

Car or Van, Using to Make Money

Carpenter

Carpet and Upholstery Cleaning

Cartoonist

Catering

Ceramics

Chair

Caning

Cheese Making

Childbirth Instructor

Children's Clothes

Children's Transportation Service

Chimney Sweep

Cleaning, House/Apartment/ Office

Cleaning Broker

Cleaning Service

Clip Art

Closet Organizer

Clothing and Accessories Design

Clown

Coaching

Coin Dealer

Collection Agency

Color Consultant

Columnist

Commercial Artist

Communications

Computer Animator

Computer Bulletin Board Owner

Computer Consultant

Computer Data Back-Up Service

Computer Programmer

Computer Repair

Computer Training

Computer Tutor for Children

Concert Promotion

Construction Management Consultant

Consultant, Art

Consultant, Beauty

Consultant, Business

Consultant, Color

Consultant, Computer

Consultant, Home Business

Consultant, Home Security

Consultant, Image

Consultant, Internet

Consultant, Landscaping

Consultant, Small Business

Consultant, Time Management

Consultant, Wedding

Contractor Referral Service

Cooking School

Co-Op Coupons

Copy Service

Copywriter, Online

Correspondence Club

Cosmetics Sales

Cosmetologist

Costume Design

Coupon Books

Crafts

Craft Broker

Crafts

Instructor

Craft Supplies Catalog

Credit and Debt Counselling Service

(D)

Dance Instructor

Dating and Escort Service

Daycare Center

Daycare for Adults

Dental Claims Processing

Designer Pet Houses

Desktop Publishing

Desktop Video

Dinner Delivery Service

Directory Publisher

Direct Sales

Disk Duplication

Diversity Consultant

Dog Trainer

Dog Walker

Doll Maker

Doula

Dressmaking/Sewing

Dried Floral Arrangements

Dry Cleaning Pick-Up and Delivery
Service

(E)

Editor

Elder Services

Email

Processing

Embossed Stationery

Employee Trainer

Employment Agency

Engineering Consultant

Errand Service

Event Management

Event Planner

Executive Search

Expert Services Broker

Expert Witness

Export Agent

Exterminator

Ezine Publishing

(F)

Facialist

Family Tree Researcher

Filing Systems

Finance Broker

Financial Advisor

Financial Planner

Firewood Supply

Fishing Supplies

Fish Tank/Bird Cage
Maintenance and Sales

Fitness Trainer

Flea Market Seller

Floral Arrangements

Foley Artist

Food Delivery Service

Forum Manager

Framing (Picture) Service

Franchise Consultant

Franchise Owner

Freebie Ad Magazines

Free Give-Aways

Freelance Artist

Freelance Photographer

Freelance Writer

Fundraiser

Furniture Restoration and
    Refurbishment

(G)

Garage Sales

Garage Sales Promotion

Garden Consultant

Gardener

Genealogist

Ghost Writer

Gift Baskets

Gift Baskets, Gourmet

Give-Aways

Gourmet Jam and Jelly

Grant Proposal Consultant

Grant Proposal Writer

Graphic Artist

Greenhouse

Greeting Cards

Greeting Card Sending Service

Grocery Shopping Service

(H)

Hairdresser

Handmade Soaps

Handyman/woman Service

Hauling Service

Healthcare Consultant

Herbalist

Herb and Spice Business

Herb Gardener

Herb Wreaths and Crafts

Home Accessories Sales

Home Business Consultant

Home Decorating

Home Furnishings

Home Healthcare Agency

Home Inspection Service

Home-Made Booklets

Home-Made Foods

Home Maintenance

Home Office Organizer

Home Organizer

Home Plan Designer

Home Security Consultant

Home Swapping Registry

Horse Boarding

Horse Exerciser

Hospital Bill Auditing

Household Management

Housekeeper

House Sitting Registry

House-Sitting Service

Housewares

"How-To" Videos

Human Resources Consultant

(I)

Image Consultant

Image Transfer

Import/Export

Imprinting

Independent Contractor

Indoor Environmental Tester

Indoor Fountains

Information Broker

Infopreneur

Insurance Sales

Internet Consultant

Interior Decorating

International Consultant

Internet Marketing

Internet Recruiting

Internet Service Provider

Interpreter/Translator

Inventory Taping Service

Invitation Printing

(J)

Jewelry, Wire

Jewelry Designer

Junk Car Removal

(L)

Lamaze Instructor

Landscaping Consultant

Landscaping Service

Laundry Service

Lawn Maintenance

Lawn Mower and Motor Repair

Lawn Sign Rentals

Leadlighting

Legal Transcription Service

Limousine Service

Lingerie Sales

Locating Service

Locksmith

Long Distance Telecommunications
   Products

(M)

Magician

Mailing List Service

Mail House

Mailing List Services

Mail Order

Make-Up Artist

Management Consultant

Manicurist

Marketing Consultant

Market Research

Massage Therapy

Matchmaker Service

Meals for Handicapped

Medical Billing

Medical Claims Processing

Medical Coding

Medical Office Consultant

Medical Transcription Service

Meeting and Event Planner

Menu Planner

Microfarming

Mini-blind Cleaning Service

Mobile Car Wash/Detailing Service

Mobile Disc Jockey

Mobile Manicurist

Mobile Notary Public

Mobile Pet Groomer

Mobile Puppet Theater

Monogramming

Moving Service

Music

Music Lessons

Mystery Shopper

(N)

Name Certificates

Nanny Finding Service

Nature Hikes

New Media/Multimedia Production

New-Mom Care

Newsletter Production for Clients

Newsletter Publishing

Newspaper Clipping Service

Notary Public

Nutritional Supplements Sales

(O)

Office Organizer

Office Plant Care

Office Support Service

Online Internet Training

Online Newspaper

Online Researcher/Abstractor

Online Retailer

Outdoor Adventures

(P)

Packing/Unpacking Service

Painting

Paper Recycling

Paralegal

Party Catering

Party Planner

Party Plan Sales

Payroll Service

Personal Chef

Personal Fitness Trainer

Personalized Stationery

Personal Shopper

Personal Sports Scorecards

Pet Breeding

Pet Fashions

Pet Food and Supplies Delivery

Pet Grooming Service

Pet Hotel

Pet Matching Service

Pet Photography Service

Pet Products

Pet Show Business

Pet Sitting/Home-Care Service

Petting Zoo Owner

Pet Transportation

Pet Walking

Photos, 3-D

Photos to Video, Transferring

Photography

Photography, sce-

nic (for homesick expats)

Piano Tuner

Picture Framing

Plant Nursery

Polling/Surveying

Pool Cleaning

Portrait and Wedding Photography

Portrait Artist

Potted Plants

Poultry Farmer

Pregnancy Fitness Class

Printing Business, Small

Printing Broker

Printer Toner Recharging

Printing, Invitations

Private Investigator

Private Practice Consultant

Process Server

Product Assembly

Product Development Consultant

Professional Organizer

Proofreader

Property Damage Appraisal Service

Property Manager

Proposal Consultant

Public Relations Agency

Public Relations Specialist

Public Speaker

(R)

Real Estate Appraiser

Real Estate Magazine

Realtor

Recipe Collections

Referral Service

Relocation Consultant

Reminder Service

Remodeling Contractor

Reporter

Restaurant Booking Service

Restaurant Delivery Service

Resume Writing Service

Retail Consultant

Reunion Organizer

Reviewer

Risk Management Consultant

River Rafting Guide

Roommate Finding Service

Rubber Stamps

(S)

Safety Consultant

School Photographer

Screen Printing

Scopist

Secretarial Service

Secret Shopper

Security Consultant

Security Video Service

Self Defense Instructor

Self-Improvement Seminars

Self Publishing

Seminars and Workshops

Seminar Promotion

Seniors Exercise Classes

Sewing/Dressmaking

Shareware Programmer

Sharpening Service

Shopping Service

Show Promoting

Shuttle Service

Sightseeing Tours

Sign Design and Painting

Sign Language Interpreter

Singer

Small Business Consultant

Snow Removal Service

Software Creation

Software Trainer

Song Writer

Speakers Agency

Special Event Videos

Specialty Consultant

Stained Glass

(T)

Tarot Reader

Tax Return Preparation Service

Teaching

Technical Writer

Telemarketing

Telephone Answering Service

Telephone Service Reseller

Temporary Help Agency

3-D Photos

Time Management Consultant

Tool Rental Service

Tour Guide

Training

Transferring Photos to Video

Translation Service

Transcript Digesting Service

Transcription Services

Translator/Interpreter

Travel Agency

Travel Agency, Specialty

Travel Club

T-Shirt Design

 Tupperware Sales

Tutoring

TV Repair

Typing Service

(U)

Used Cars

Used CDs

Using Your Car or Van to Make Money

Utility Auditing

(V)

Vacation House Swap Service

Vending Machine Business

VCR Repair

Video Duplication Service

Video Taping Service

Vitamin/Nutrition/Weight

Loss Product Sales

Voicemail

Voice Instructor

Voice Over

(W)

Website Design

Website Development

Web Hosting Services

Web Marketing

Wedding Consultant

Wedding Coordinator

Wedding Planner

Wedding Video Service

Welcoming Service

Window Washing Service

Windshield Repair

Woodworking

Word Processing

Workshops, Seminars and

Writing Audio Cassette Scripts

Writing Press Releases

(Y)

Yard Clean Up

Proverbs 37:25

I have been young, and now old; yet I have not seen the righteous forsaken, nor his seed begging bread.

www.ingramcontent.com/pod-product-compliance
Lightning Source LLC
Chambersburg PA
CBHW071258130626
46556CB00003B/1362